One
Silver
Second

A Fable for All Ages

by Daphne Doward Hogstrom
illustrated by Gordon Laite

Rand McNally & Company
Chicago / New York / San Francisco

Library of Congress Cataloging in Publication Data

Hogstrom, Daphne Doward.
  One silver second.

    SUMMARY: As each animal cultivates a voice that fits
his personality, he forgets the common voice that once allowed
all animals to talk and live together in friendship and peace.
    [1. Animals—Stories] I. Laite, Gordon, illus.
II. Title.
PZ10.3.H702On   [Fic]   71-174641
ISBN 0-528-82188-1
ISBN 0-528-82189-X (lib. bdg.)

First printing, July, 1972

*For all my
    beautiful children*

ONCE UPON A TIME, all the birds and beasts of the world spoke with the same kind of voice. The sound of it was something between a purr and a churr and a trill. And all the birds and animals talked happily together and lived with each other in friendship and peace.

But, one day, the lion looked at himself in the lake. Seeing his long, brown body and his strong, white teeth, he thought:

"Why should a big, brawny fellow like myself talk with a purr and a churr and a trill? I should be growling and yowling and roaring like the wind! I should have a fine, fierce voice to match my fine, fierce appearance!"

And the lion hurried off to Mumbo Max, the mad magician of the forest, sitting in his house of leaves.

Mumbo Max waved a few wands and blew a few whistles, and soon the lion ran back to his den growling and yowling and roaring like the wind!

Next, the elephant looked at himself in the water. Seeing a great, gray body and a large, leathery trunk, he thought:

"Why should a great, grand fellow like myself talk with a purr and a churr and a trill? I should have a strong, stout voice to match my strong, stout appearance!"

And off he hurried to Mumbo Max, sitting in his house of leaves.

Mumbo Max waved a few wands and blew a
few whistles, and soon the elephant was rushing
through the trees, huffing and puffing and trumpet-
ing like a storm!

Next, the tiger grew unhappy with his voice.

"I am a lean, long, handsome beast," he thought. "Why should I talk with a purr and a churr and a trill? I should have a bold, brave voice to match my bold, brave looks." And off he marched to Mumbo Max in the forest.

Soon, he was bounding through the grasses, grumping and grunting and growling in the night.

Then the wolf became unhappy. He, too, went to Mumbo Max in the forest.

He came back, yelping and yapping and baying at the moon.

One by one, all the animals followed suit. One
by one, each went to visit Mumbo Max in the forest.
The dog returned barking and blaring.
The turkey returned gabbling and gobbling.
The lamb returned baaing and bleating.
The monkey returned chittering and chattering.
The cat returned mewing and meowing.

The robin returned peeping and cheeping.
The horse returned neighing.
The mule returned braying.
The duck returned quacking.
The hen returned clacking.
The cock returned crowing.
The cow returned lowing.

And even the tiniest mouse came back with a
squeak and a screech and a squeal!

At last, all the birds and animals had changed their voices, until only the dove remained.

"Why should I change my voice?" she thought, looking at herself in the lake. "I am soft and white and simple, and my gentle voice exactly matches my gentle appearance."

And she continued to talk with her calm, quiet "coo"—which was something between a purr and a churr and a trill!

But the other birds and beasts soon forgot the sound of their old voices, and could not talk to her any more.

Nor could they talk to one another.

Sometimes they honked and gronked at each other.

Sometimes they snorted and snarled.

Sometimes they bellowed and bawled at each other.

And sometimes they FOUGHT!

"I have lost my feathers to the fox!" squawked the chicken. "I wish we were friends once again."

"I have lost my whiskers to the wildcat!" squealed the rabbit. "I wish we were friends once again."

"And everyone runs when I roar!" howled the lion. "If only we were friends once again!"

And for the second time the animals grew unhappy. For the second time they went to Mumbo Max in the middle of the forest.

But Mumbo Max had long ago left. Hearing all the squabbling and squalling, he had picked up his books and bottles, packed up his wands and whistles, and disappeared over the mountains in a cloud of smoke!

Only a heap of brown dust—all that was left of his house of leaves—remained to tell the animals that he had once lived amongst them.

"How can we be friends now?" thought the lamb, looking at the wolf.

"How can we be friends now?" thought the wolf, looking at the lamb.

"Coo," said the dove, with a purr and a churr and a little, soft trill.

And, for one silver second, all the birds and
beasts of the earth lifted their heads, listened, and
remembered—and the forest was filled with friendship, and the world was filled with peace.